# The Dirty Thirty

*I travel The Dirty Thirty alone, searching for something, searching for myself.*

*What I don't expect to find is him.*

By Jessa Kaye

Copyright © 2014 by Jessa Kaye

Edited by Fran Walsh, Ali Maki and Rachel Lawrence

*Summary: Distraught over her impending thirtieth birthday and encouraged by a new, mysterious friend, Sydney Harper decides to strike out on an adventure, leaving her dismal life behind. With nothing but a suitcase in her hand and the wind on her back, she hitchhikes across The Dirty Thirty, checking off a list of hopes and dreams as she travels the highway, and discovering something she never expected.*

*She finds herself. She finds him.*

*This story is a work of fiction. Names, characters, businesses, places, events, and incidents are either the product of the author's imagination or used in a fictitious manner. Any resemblance to actual persons, living or dead, or actual events is purely coincidental.*

*Warning: This novella contains several explicit scenes of an erotic, sexual nature. This story is intended for adults over the age of eighteen. All characters portrayed are eighteen or older.*

*Special thanks to L.C. Morgan, whose birthday and unwavering friendship was the inspiration behind this novella. Thanks to author Allyn Lesley for pre-reading The Dirty Thirty and for offering your abundant suggestions. Special thanks to Fran, who originally edited this work of fiction while it still lived in the Twilight world. Thanks to Ali Maki and Rachel Lawrence for your editing work during the transitional phase of this story.*

*Thanks to my husband who gave me the room to breathe and type while not complaining ... much. And to my lovely children who say, "All Mama does is peck-peck-peck on her laptop." Hopefully all my "pecking" hasn't been in vain.*

*But most of all, I thank my readers and the fandom for rekindling the fire inside my heart. Thank you for reminding me that I was once a thirteen-year-old girl with a typewriter and a dream. I lost her somewhere along the way. She's missed me, just as much as I've missed her.*

Cover Art © L.J. Anderson, Mayhem Cover Creations

# Chapter One

There is nothing unpredictable or chaotic about my life. Each day is an endless routine of mundane bullshit that makes me want to slit my wrists.

I wake up every morning alone in my bed. There's no husband, no boyfriend, no significant other—unless you count my vibrator who I spend more time with than anyone I know. Although I'm quite fond of my phallus-shaped friend, I doubt he'd make for interesting dinner conversation the way a significant other would.

After waking up I yawn and head to the bathroom to pee. Then I wash my hands and brush my teeth. While the coffee brews, I slink out to the end of the driveway in my pajamas to retrieve the newspaper. The kid who delivers it seems to always toss it in the motherfucking bushes. Half the time it's there hidden among the tiny, glossy, green leaves, and the other half the neighbor's dog has chewed it up, scattering the black and white printed pages across my dewy lawn.

I really hate that damn dog.

Once inside, I pour myself a cup of coffee. I take it black.

Then I spend the next few minutes frying bacon and eggs, inevitably burning each because my cooking is shit. It's one *skill* I *learned* on my own. Growing up without a mother, I was raised by my father, a man who ordered takeout for us every night for the entire eighteen years I lived with him. I'll probably be diabetic in a few years. It's either that or die of heart disease from all the greasy meals I've consumed in my life.

My thoughts have taken a rather morbid turn lately as I'm closing in on thirty. I feel the inevitable day creeping up. It's almost as though I can see the years slowly dwindling by, and it's killing me that I have accomplished nothing in my life.

Nothing.

I dreamed of going to college when I was younger, and managed to do so for a while, living off student loans and grants, but the money quickly ran out. The bills began to pile up and I found myself working not only one full time job in the evenings, but a part time job as well, just to make it in the world on my own. My grades began slipping, and the next thing I knew I was on academic probation until they deteriorated to the point where I lost my scholarship. Things only went downhill from there.

Eventually I let it all go. The stress outweighed my drive to succeed. With each passing day, I hated myself a little more for the mistakes made in my youth. I'd suddenly become my mother, a woman who never finished anything she set out to do in life, a woman who accomplished no goals, and gave up on everything.

Being a wife.

Being a mother.

Sometimes I find myself wondering about the woman who birthed me, a woman my father claims I could be the ghost of. Besides sharing the same DNA and the same lack of motivation, we also mirror each other in appearance. She's still there, her image tucked in the back of my mind and on the scratched and faded photographs I sometimes remove from a bookshelf in my bedroom. The matted paper with her unsmiling face is damaged from time and the occasional tear. Long, dirty-blonde hair and lifeless blue eyes stoically stare back at me during the times I shuffle through the photos. How my father didn't recognize her unhappiness, I'll never know. At nearly the same age she was when she left us behind, I'm mature enough to notice the despondency in her face, the slump of her shoulders, the way she stood to the side of me in the photographs. In the handful of photos with her holding me, she still looked unhappy.

Stiff.

Cold.

Uncaring.

*What made her so unhappy? Was it because of me? Is it my fault she left us? Am I the reason for her asphalt-coated heart?*

The smell of burning toast drags me from my internal reverie. I shuffle over to the oven because I'm too broke to afford a toaster since I blew up the last one. I pull the slightly burned toast from the rack, cringing at the blackened crust. The next five minutes are spent scraping the bottom of the bread. Each swipe of the butter knife against the bread grates on my nerves, and I take turns cringing and sighing in frustration.

This is my life.

My eyes drift to the open window over the sink while I continue scraping, peppering the shiny silver surface below with the charred mess. Kids ride their bikes down the tiny road. They laugh and sing, teasing each other. The girls speed away from the quickly pursuing boys, their faces aflame with embarrassment and their skirts flapping wildly in the wind. Their knobby-kneed legs pedal anxiously, and I wonder when I last felt that carefree.

When was the last time I felt that exuberant over being pursued by a man?

When was the last time I relished in the brilliancy of the wind slapping my reddened cheeks?

I shake my head and throw my burned toast on a plate, slather some jelly on it and stuff my face until I'm miserable. The sadness lingers, but it is muffled now, partly snuffed out by a full belly and the reluctance of another day at work.

***

I tried waiting tables. I applied for a job at Lloyd's, a local truck stop just off *The Dirty Thirty* in the tiny, rainy town of Flint, Oregon. I started working at Lloyd's when I was nineteen years old. I never could grasp waitressing.

Literally.

I could never *grasp* anything.

The plates perched on my arms would tilt this way and that, spilling fries on customers' laps. Cokes landed on the floor, splashing against the stained tile. The other waitresses, the more seasoned, established ones, would shake their heads in shame at my antics, their eyes rimmed in pity. Their sympathy only pissed me off. It pissed me off that I couldn't do something as simple as delivering a few plates of food to a table without it being a complete and utter disaster.

I was quickly demoted to dishwasher.

Almost eleven years have passed since then. I've been scraping and scrubbing and spraying food from dirty dishes for nearly eleven years. I do it even now, and as I watch the suds disappear down the drain, I realize these suds are a metaphor for my motherfucking life.

The panic builds inside my chest. Is this it? Is this all I deserve out of life? Is this the cruel hand God has dealt me? I'm to grow old alone, living in some shitty nowhere town for the rest of my days, too broke to afford a fucking toaster?

I want more.

There are things I've always wanted to do but have yet to do them. I've always been responsible Sydney, the girl in high school who studied on the weekends instead of partying with her friends. I was the girl who dated the good, sensible guys, the type of men my father approved of, yet bored me to tears. What's come of it?

Nothing.

At the end of my shift I shuffle into the bathroom, glancing briefly in the mirror as I run my fingers through my deep, dirty-blonde hair. My fingers pause in the lackluster strands, caught in the frizzy mess caused by bending over steaming hot water in a greasy kitchen all day.

My blue eyes are dead. They're dead just like this town.

Dead like my love life.

Dead like my future.

The tears don't spill over until I'm in the back parking lot, bending, hands on knees near the back dumpster having a full-blown panic attack.

That's where I find her.

Maybe that's where she finds me.

I hear her before I see her. Her strangled grunts and muffled curses sound out above the scuffle of feet and heckling of dirty old men. I'll later wonder if this girl is an angel, although I'm sure she's not. I'll even question if she's real. Maybe she's the voice of reason buried somewhere in the back of my mind. Either way, she's in the parking lot behind the shitty diner where I work getting attacked by three grown men as they try to pin her against the side of the neighboring brick building and accost her.

The woman is around my age or maybe a bit younger, wearing black leather chaps, a wife beater and a leather vest. Her exposed arms are covered in tattoos, and her long, raven hair is in a wild, windswept disarray. I'm unable to focus on any other fine details.

As two of the men pin her arms against the building, I'm shocked into stunned silence as the remaining man grasps her wife beater between his beefy fingers, ripping it halfway down the front of her chest. I find myself fumbling blindly inside my cheap, pleather purse, searching for the one thing my overprotective father always insisted I carry. I breathe a sigh of relief as I find my trusty Taser. Turns out, I don't even have to use it.

Before I can bat an eye, the guy standing in front of the woman is curled in the fetal position on the dirty ground, clutching his abdomen, or maybe his groin. The two men pinning her against the wall automatically let go as they watch their friend fall. Each one is assaulted with the spiked heel of the woman's pointy, black boots.

Blood flies from their faces, their heads snapping back with each strike of her boot. The woman never stops. She never pauses for a breath. She kicks and hits and punches and screams obscenities until all three men are joined together in a pile on the asphalt, moaning and groaning in pain, twisted in a bloody mess as she sneers at them.

I blink.

"You got anything to eat in there?" the woman asks, nodding her head toward the restaurant. "Been a long ride and I'm starving."

The voice that comes out of her mouth is low, raspy and sexy. As she removes a cigarette from a crumpled packet in the front pocket of her vest, I immediately know why. I nod numbly, my fingers fumbling once again in my purse. I drop the Taser inside and pull out a set of keys. The woman follows me, laughing as I quietly explain there is a new non-smoking policy inside the old building.

She blows smoke in the air and raises an eyebrow. Her blatant disregard for the diner rules perturbs me, but instead of calling her on it, I drop my gaze to the keys in my hand.

"I'll call the cops about those assholes," I say.

I unlock the back door, allow her pass me by then quickly lock the door behind us. The woman nods, pausing only to grab a clean glass from a drying rack and dump her ashes inside. She explores the back room, even opening the large refrigerator to disappear inside, emerging with a grin and a giant tub of chocolate chip cookie dough.

I watch her with wide eyes and the phone pressed to my ear. She helps herself to a spoon and saunters into the dark dining area, switching on the lights as she enters the room.

After ending the call, I join her. I find her sitting on top of a table, legs crossed beneath her, shoving spoonful after spoonful of cookie dough into her mouth. I approach the odd woman slowly and quietly, almost as though she's a wild, wounded animal.

She very well may be.

"The police are on their way."

The woman nods thoughtfully at my statement. Her eyes are fixed on something, yet nothing, in the distance. Their warm, dark depths seem to be remembering something from long ago.

As I slide onto a nearby chair staring at her, I find myself wanting to know more about this strange woman. I want to know why she was hanging out in the dark parking lot of a shitty truck stop in the middle of nowhere. I *need* to know how a small person such as herself learned to kick, hit and punch the way she did.

"Where did you learn all those moves?" I take a deep breath. My chest feels tight. "Why were you in the back lot?"

"You worked here a while?" Ignoring my question, she drops the container of cookie dough carelessly beside her, fixing her eyes on mine.

"Since I was nineteen," I respond, my eyes flitting across her vest and the various patches fixed therein. "Ten years. Almost eleven years."

She tilts her head to the side. "You like working here?"

I contemplate her question for a moment before letting out a dry, bitter laugh.

"No. No, I don't like working here."

"So, why do you?" she asks seriously, studying me closely. "Work here, I mean."

My bottom lip is wedged between my teeth.

The question is so simple, yet so complex.

Why *do* I work somewhere that obviously makes me so unhappy? Why do I subject myself to this miserable life day after day?

"What else would I do?" I ask, shrugging as the sound of police sirens suddenly wail in the distance.

"Whatever makes you happy."

I mull over her words for a long moment, her gaze weighing heavily on mine.

"Do you always do what makes *you* happy?"

Smirking, she slides off the tabletop and gives me a wink. I follow her to the back door, my sneakers scuffling against the sticky linoleum.

"Always," she says before disappearing through the back door.

# Chapter Two

Ellie Jackson, the girl I met in the dark parking lot of the truck stop, is a selfish little thing. She reveals so little about herself, yet becomes completely absorbed in my pathetic excuse of a life, drinking up everything I have to say like a woman dying of thirst. She knows all my hopes, my dreams, my fears. I share the pain of having a mother who brought me into the world yet found me so inconsequential that she never took the time to care anything for me. I tell her about growing up as the only child of an emotionally stunted man and of the loneliness I felt. She knows every failed relationship I've had over the years, and how not one man found me interesting enough to stick around for very long.

Ellie becomes a fixture in my life, until one day, she isn't.

"You're doing the right thing, Sydney." She slings my suitcase in the backseat of my beat-up car.

"This is the most dangerous decision I've ever made."

"It is." She nods, her long, straight bangs falling into her eyes.

"I could die."

"Possibly," she says, "but were you ever really alive to begin with?"

I say nothing. She continues.

"To die at twenty-nine ... to be in your twenties forever, it's a romantic concept, no?"

*Um, no.*

"Ellie, you're psychotic."

"Yet you listen to me." She giggles, her slight Southern drawl endearing. "You're taking my advice. Do you have the list?"

I do.

It's the only thing in my possession besides the suitcase with a few changes of clothes, a toothbrush, toothpaste, a loaded twenty-two, my Taser, my cell and an assortment of feminine hygiene products. I wave the folded napkin in the air, blushing as I remember the things listed on the thin, wrinkled paper.

"Don't be embarrassed, Syd." Ellie throws her leg over her motorcycle and guns the engine, yelling her last words over the rumbling machine quaking beneath her. "You still have time to cross one wish off your list."

Ellie pats the bike with a grin, and I hesitantly shake my head.

"I'm not ready for that yet." A knot of fear swells inside my chest, working itself up and lodging inside my throat.

I've always been terrified, yet mesmerized by motorcycles. It is one of my many dreams, to ride a motorcycle on the open road. I want to feel what those kids felt on their bicycles the day I stared at them through my dirty kitchen window. I'd take it. I'd take the freedom and exhilaration; just not right now.

I'm not ready and it somehow doesn't feel *right* riding with Ellie.

"Do you have the envelope?" she asks.

The heel of her boot shoves the kickstand back as she heaves the huge bike up. I pat one of the front pockets of my shorts. The stiff paper of the envelope pokes the tender skin residing below.

"Yes," I whisper.

She notices the worry I'm sure is reflecting on my face, and for a brief moment she looks hesitant. My new friend, my *only* friend, is leaving me. She's leaving me standing next to my shitty car in my shitty driveway in this shitty, little town, and I don't know if I'll ever see her again.

"When do I open it?" I ask. "When do I open the envelope?"

Ellie grins, revving the engine once more and licking her lips.

"Open it when you're ready to reach your destination."

Before I know it she's gone, rumbling down the dirty road on the long, sleek motorcycle, leaving nothing but exhaust in her wake. I watch her dark silhouette until I can't see it anymore, blinded by the strain of the sun on my weary eyes.

I sigh as her silhouette is swallowed by the sunset.

Sliding onto the worn seat of my car, I muse over my new direction in life, remembering the confusion and disbelief in my father's eyes as I head in the direction of The Dirty Thirty. He hadn't believed me, not for one minute, when I told him I was quitting the truck stop.

Abandoning my job was never in my plans, but I'd worked there for years, not once taking a vacation. I asked for twenty-nine days, three months in advance. The manager had three months to give me what I needed: twenty-nine days for twenty-nine years of my miserable life. Yet Mark Lloyd, manager and owner of the crappy truck stop, turned me down flat, bumbling and fumbling over the excuse of not having anyone to replace me, which was shit. I didn't give a damn if he *himself* had to get his hands wet with dirty dishwater. I needed a break.

So I took it. A permanent one.

I flung a dish towel in his face and walked away the day I quit. I was angry at first and then giddy with the excitement of doing something I'd never done before, quitting a job without notice. Quitting a job without notice was something responsible Sydney wouldn't do. No, responsible Sydney would mull it over for a few days before making a concrete decision.

Responsible Sydney doesn't do anything abruptly.

Responsible Sydney is sensible.

Responsible Sydney no longer exists.

Once I convinced my father that I truly did quit and had no set-in-stone plans for my future, he'd shoved a wad of cash in my hands, smiling shyly at the stunned look on my face. He quietly explained it was emergency money he'd saved up for hard times. I took the money after much insistence on his part, not being the type of woman who'd ever easily accepted handouts from anyone.

Now I'm sitting here on the bypass, swallowing the thickness forming inside my throat, staring at the cars and trucks flying by. Smoke billows from beneath the hood, the stench of what smells like burning rubber assaulting my nostrils. With my hands grasping the steering wheel in a chokehold, my head falls back against the headrest of the seat. Hysterical laughter bubbles inside of me, the fucking irony of the entire situation striking me the way an untrained child strikes the keys on a piano—sudden and with giddy anticipation. I was already planning on ditching my car on the side of the road before taking this journey. No sense in pretending my less than dependable automobile would ever take me far out of town. Hell, it barely got me to work and back as it is.

*A smoking engine is just another reason to leave this broken-down piece of shit car behind.*

For the first time ever, a strange sense of predestination washes over me. Some people are awed by the discovery of hidden treasures, some by the grace of

God once they find religion. Me? I'm wonderstruck by a blown head gasket.

After catching my breath, I sigh and climb out of the car. Slamming the squeaky, protesting door behind me, I wish I had something monumental or symbolic to say to the old vehicle, but find nothing. The truth is I hate this fucking car with its smoking engine, just like I hate this fucking life I'm living.

So I leave the car behind on the side of the road. I climb the embankment of the overpass, wading through overgrown grass and the weeds clinging to my legs, stomping wildflowers beneath my worn shoes.

I walk The Dirty Thirty with the sun on my back and my thumb in the air, heading somewhere far, far away from here.

\*\*\*

There are only a few things from my list I cross out as I travel the highway, but there are tons of things I do that I never dreamed of doing along the way as well.

In Idaho I consume a baked potato as big as my head. The older men inside the dim diner egg me on, causing me to giggle like a child. I'm scowling at them later, not only because of my pained, protruding belly, but because the potato wasn't just one, but two potatoes cleverly arranged to look like one.

The potato-picking bastards tricked me.

I ride a horse in Nebraska, a feat that doesn't sound overwhelmingly exciting to many, yet is altogether terrifying and thrilling to me, a girl who grew up afraid of her own shadow. I smile as the sun sets in the distance, the evidence of my incredible achievement shifting his feet below. The coarse tail of the animal lazily whips through the air, the strands languidly slapping against my leg as he softly neighs.

I make love to a man in Indiana, lying on a quilt thicker than the blanket of stars sparkling in the celestial sky overhead. Crickets sing a shrill song around us, their cries fading away and replaced by our own. The man calls me by another woman's name, murmuring the word as a tear slips down his sun-kissed cheek. I allow it and even find no offense in being called by the wrong name. For as blissfully pleasurable as it feels to have him buried deep inside me, it still doesn't feel completely right.

It's *never* felt completely right.

His shuddering body relaxes, his length softening inside me. He places one last kiss to the corner of my mouth and curls beside me atop the patchwork cotton. I begin to feel restless and hollow, once again alone in the world, even with the big brute of a man resting so close by. The excitement of the past few days has worn away. As the man falls asleep, I slip from his arms, digging around in my suitcase until I find the wrinkled envelope my strange friend handed me before she drove out of my life.

I slip my finger beneath the flap and break the seal. There's a folded note hidden inside. Removing the scrap of paper with shaky fingers, I'm slightly nervous to find what Ellie has written.

Scrawled across the paper is an address in Biloxi, Mississippi. There's no explanation, no phone number. There's just an address written in black ink, the words and numbers written bold and perfect, just like her.

There's a key inside as well. It's simple and gold, slightly muddled from age. There are no numbers engraved on it. The surface is smooth and dull. I hold it in the air against the sun, as though it's the key to *everything*, the key to my happiness, the key to my future, and maybe it is. The thought brings a wistful smile to my face.

The next day I take a detour.

I leave The Dirty Thirty.

Abandoning the elusive highway feels symbolic in a way I didn't feel when leaving my car behind, the car I'd had for years. Leaving The Dirty Thirty, a road I had never traveled before, isn't only like leaving a highway behind, but leaving my age behind as well.

Fuck thirty.

I'm twenty-nine.

Maybe it's just for a number of weeks, but I'm still fucking twenty-nine.

I leave Indiana behind, never looking back.

***

My trip isn't completely smooth.

I'm attacked in Tennessee, held down by a truck driver who wants a little more from me than I'm willing to give. It's the one and only time I ever use my father's gun, other than target practice, but thankfully I don't kill the man.

The girl writhing beneath him with a gun pressed against his temple and eyes wide with shock and anger is enough to make him back off. I leave him on the side of the road and walk for miles, too scared to accept a ride from anyone until my feet hit Mississippi soil. Overcome with exhaustion and aching from the overused muscles in my calves and thighs, I reach a breaking point, willing to take a ride from just about anyone.

An old man in a faded, blue pickup truck pulls to the side of the road and offers me a ride. I accept, grateful for the kind, watery eyes greeting me as I slide into the musty cab. I ask him to drop me off somewhere near the closest used car dealership.

I'm thankful for the man's silence as we ride along. The only sound is the wind whipping in through the open windows and the gritty voice of Johnny Cash quietly crooning from the cracked speakers. Lack of conversation gives me an opportunity to be reflective of my time on the road, of the incident that happened in Tennessee and of the wonder and excitement of what I'll find in Biloxi. It's a place I've never been, and have never cared to see.

Until now.

The old man leaves me just where I asked, in the parking lot of a used car lot, which looks more like a junkyard situated in the middle of a ghost town. I wave at the truck puttering away in the distance. He throws one wrinkled, weathered arm through the window, returning the silent gesture.

I purchase a VW bug with some of my dad's emergency money. The car is rusty and red with chipped paint and a dented bumper, but it has a convertible top.

I've dreamed of owning a convertible since hitting puberty it seems, but I'd always talked myself out of buying one. Convertible tops get worn and frayed, causing leaks on rainy days and eventually have to be replaced, which is expensive, not to mention impractical in Oregon. But when I close my eyes and imagine myself driving around some obscure, Southern beach town during the remainder of the summer, all the cons billow away with the humid breeze.

When I slip inside I feel like a teenager again, yet not the teenager I once was. I feel like the kid I *should have* been, happy and carefree, grinning with the top laid back. Peeling down the heat-cracked highway, I breathe in the alluring smell of magnolias and pink mimosas blowing in the breeze.

In no real hurry, a couple of days pass before I reach my destination. I break down and pay for a hotel room both days. Basking in the Mississippi sun, I sip sweet tea and lie on a lounge chair beside the hotel pool with my head tipped back. I close my eyes against the sun, my heavy lids protected from the bright light. I think of nothing for two days.

I think of nothing for the first time in my life.

# Chapter Three

I arrive in Biloxi on a Friday. I don't immediately go to the address Ellie so covertly led me to. Instead, I sit on the beach for a while. The sun hangs in the air, the wavering lines of heat dancing below the fiery globe and disappearing into the dark water, like a melting scoop of orange sherbet wasting away on the pavement. The waves of the Gulf are nothing like the ones I witnessed on the shores of Oregon. The water is a different color, as is the sand, and I find that I love the Gulf of Mexico.

I love the sounds of excited children running the length of the beach.

I love that I don't have to worry about a downpour at any given moment.

I love the casinos and gambling and rednecks in cheap suits sipping whiskey.

I love the smell of fried food mixed with ice cream wafting from the many stores. And I love the cheap souvenirs, seagull picture frames and sand dollar Christmas ornaments.

I wonder why Ellie left this place, why she traveled all the way from Biloxi to Oregon. I wonder if she was escaping something as well. The thought of my mysterious friend constantly searching for something in life, yet never discovering it, saddens me. So I push the thought aside, along with the sand between my toes, as I stand. I find my car in the throng of vehicles far from the shore and pull out the map I found earlier in the glove box.

I leave the beach behind.

I leave the sun and the waves and the parasailers drifting across the clear blue sky. The map pinned between my hands and the steering wheel flaps in the breeze. The smell of the salty Gulf slowly fades away. I take the back roads, disappearing beneath the lingering pines and strong oaks. The road I travel winds around, twisting this way and that, shielding my view of anything other than green leaves and thick brush, until I see it ahead.

A lake.

A seemingly never-ending lake surrounded by spaced-out wooden houses with large windows and wrap-around decks overlooking the dirty waters below. Piers jut from the land in front of the homes. Kids climb tall, winding slides from the shore, squealing as they slide down and plunge into the murky water. I shudder slightly, the thought of the dark waters and what lies beneath them causing me to cringe. It's on my list ... one of the many things on my list. I want to learn how to swim. I want to feel light and weightless, just as Ellie had vividly described to me, her arms flailing about, as I shared my secret desire to learn a skill most people my age already know.

A memory of a torrid ocean floods my mind, one with my mother standing at my side staring into the angry waves. Even after all these years, I remember every detail of how my mother looked that day. The memory is as crisp and hauntingly beautiful as my mother herself, with her hair whipping in the wind and the high-waisted, sweetheart top bikini gracing her with an old world style allure. With feet sunken in the sand, the waves lapping at her toes, a ghost of a smile turned her lips. But then she turned, meeting my curious gaze from where I sat in the sand, a bucket and shovel sitting between my idle legs. Her smile was gone just as quickly as it appeared, washed away with the tide she sunk into as she ignored my quiet request to teach me how to swim.

Shaking off the memory, I focus on the road ahead. When I reach my destination I park the car and stare up at the monstrosity in front of me, my mouth slightly ajar. The wooden house is huge: it has two stories with a wraparound deck on the bottom floor and a wraparound balcony on the top. The roof is made of shiny tin. I instantly imagine the sound of a rainstorm pounding against the gleaming surface, longing for a sudden downpour I so typically despised while in Oregon.

The image of the rain pattering against the tin roof, lulling me to sleep in front of the picture windows overlooking the lake is tempting. I find myself slipping from the car, blindly slamming the door behind me as the gravel crunches beneath my feet in the drive.

The sound of engines revving and carefree laughter draws me around the house. I bypass the front door altogether, my feet sinking in the soft grass. The sight before me causes me to pause.

There's the lake, the gentle waves lapping against the shore. A stone pathway winds down the sloping hill in front of the home, ending at the shoreline. A wooden walkway also swoops down the steep hill, ending at a boat dock where a houseboat stands virtually unmoved by the soft waves slapping the sides.

Canoes are propped upside down on metal structures beneath the tall, looming trees. Teenagers on jet skis cut across the water, laughing and yelling as they ride so dangerously close to one another. Sucking in a deep breath, my heart doesn't slow to a normal rhythm until they disappear in the distance, still laughing and yelling.

The lake is so far, so wide, that it's almost impossible to see across. I strain my eyes to make out the houses in the distance, tucked neatly beneath the trees standing tall and proud in their stature.

Taking a deep breath, I pull the gold key from my jean shorts and trudge back up the hill. Once I'm standing on the shaded porch, suitcase in one hand, I slide the key inside the door, smiling as it easily opens.

I toss the suitcase on a nearby couch before exploring the house, slightly shocked to see it looks so lived in. There's a pot of coffee still sitting in the coffee maker, although I'm not sure how long it's been there. There's a little food in the fridge, but the carton of eggs I find is still in date, along with sandwich meat and a few other items. I make a mental note to head into town later and load up on my favorite carb-enriched guilty pleasures.

There's a phone perched on the bar near the kitchen. A small, orange light flashes methodically from the base, taunting me. As wrong as it may seem, I hit the button on the base, greedily listening in and gasping as I hear Ellie's raspy voice.

"If you're listening to this, Sydney, that means you made it." She chuckles. "You made it to Biloxi. You made it to my home. Stay there as long as you want to. Find a job. Don't find a job. Do something dangerous and completely irresponsible. No matter what you do, have fun doing it. And ... take care, Sydney. Take care."

There's a clicking sound as her voice fades away. I'm left wondering about her last sentence ... take care. The words sounded so hesitant, so ominous.

Backing away from the phone, I decide to explore the house. I'm confused by the loads of dirty laundry I find piled up in the living room and the blindingly obvious dirty carpet running along the wide staircase.

Shrugging, I climb the steps and glance from room to room, further confused as I find one room locked. There's another bedroom with an unkempt, messy bed that I assume is Ellie's. The color of the room is neutral, warm and inviting, but I don't want to delve inside. The thought makes me feel like an intruder in her personal space. I toss my suitcase in a seemingly unused bedroom across the hall from Ellie's and head back downstairs. Shaking my head and chuckling, I begin washing some random person's laundry, some *man's* laundry, I gather, in the living room.

I must be losing my mind ... washing some stranger's clothes.

I smile as I think of Ellie entertaining a man in her home before heading out on the open road. The clothes I'm washing must be his. Chuckling at the thought, I strip down to nothing but my bra and panties. I toss my dirty laundry, along with the clothes from my suitcase, into the wash.

The sun dips closer to the lake as I wash, dry and fold clothes, only pausing to pad to the window on occasion and peer at the peacefulness outside. I'm so absorbed in my housework that I don't hear *him* as he approaches.

"I'd ask you what the fuck you're doing in my house," a smooth voice says in my ear, his warm breath washing over me, sending goose bumps erupting across my flesh, "but it's not often I find a beautiful, half-naked woman doing my laundry, so I'm not gonna knock it."

Shrieking in shock, I spin around and find myself pinned against the washing machine by a man—a very tall, very *young* man who stares down at me with a quirked eyebrow and a teasing smile on his face.

"Should I call the cops now, or wait until you finish this load?"

"Who *are* you?" I ask, pressing myself further against the cool metal of the washing machine.

"Who am *I*?" he asks, laughing. "Who are *you*? You're in *my* house."

"Your house?" I say dumbly. I give him a good once-over for the first time, taking in his obvious youth and carefree smirk. "This is *Ellie's* house, isn't it?"

"You know Ellie?" he questions, his mirth melting away, replaced with hope and a hint of loneliness. "You're a friend of hers?"

"Yes," I whisper, feeling extremely awkward under his solemn gaze. "She's letting me stay here for a while."

The man says nothing in response. The seriousness leaves his eyes. I suck in a deep breath as he steps forward and places his hands on either side of the washer, trapping me within inches of his body. His eyes flit across my face for a moment before dipping down to my chest.

My nipples immediately harden under his gaze, because fuck, he's gorgeous. His stormy, blue eyes are intense yet playful, surrounded by thick, dark lashes. The worn shirt he wears clings to his upper body, flaunting his cut chest. He's wearing board shorts, as though he was out swimming, although they're not wet, and a pair of leather flip-flops. His skin is tan, kissed by the sun, and he smells like fuck-me-twice-and-please-come-back-for-more. His hair is wild, flopping this way and that. Freshly fucked hair, the color of sand with sun-streaked hints of gold. I immediately think of sex for the millionth time in the past few seconds I've gaped at him.

"I mean, if that's okay … me living here for a while." I sound like an idiot as the words spill from my mouth. I'm too enthralled, too dumbfounded by this man to form coherent sentences.

His gaze lingers on my breasts for a moment, a slow smile curling on his face as he notices my nipples straining against the thin fabric of my bra. I cross my arms, and my fingers accidentally graze against his *very hard* chest. The shock of this man's presence fades away and is replaced with the reality that I'm standing in his laundry room wearing nothing but my panties and bra. He leans in further, taking my breath away as his face moves so extremely close to mine, his smirk returning again.

"What's your name?" he asks.

"Sydney Harper."

"Sydney." He says my name like it's a dirty word. My thighs clench with the low grit of his voice. "Nice to meet you, Sydney. I'm Jared, and I guess we're roommates."

He draws away from me, pushing his hands against the washing machine and grinning as he saunters away. I dumbly follow him until he disappears through the laundry room door. Lingering near the doorway, I don't move again until he's walked outside. I dart across the room and stand near a window overlooking the lake. My eyes never leave his retreating frame as he walks toward the water, even long after he moves onto the pier. He peels the sinfully tight shirt from his body and dives gracefully into the water.

I watch him long into the evening. I hide behind the curtains inside the dark house until he hoists himself back on the pier, emerging from the lake, dripping with water. Then I dart upstairs, lock the door and stare at the ceiling for hours, completely exhausted, but feeling more awake, more alive, than I have my entire life.

# Chapter Four

Sharing a space with someone I don't know feels strange, moving from room to room and feeling the breath pulled out of me every time I see him, somehow forgetting this man is living in the same house as me.

Jared, on the other hand, appears completely comfortable with our sudden living situation. He chats easily with me over the next few days, explaining that Ellie is his sister, his only sibling. He talks about his job, working in construction over the summer. I watch him as he comes and goes, leaving for work with a smile on his face and returning with one as well. The smile he returns with is normally tired and sometimes a little sad, although I'm not sure why.

One day he offers to cook, laughing as I blush after ruining another meal. He suggests we go grocery shopping, rolling his eyes when I offer to pay for the groceries. Then he snatches the keys to my bug from my nimble fingers, claiming he's driving.

I let him.

Truth be known, I'll probably let him do anything—with me, to me. There's no denying the sexual attraction I have for this man. I hate myself for feeling the way I do about him, this guy who casually mentions he's eighteen years old and starting college in the fall. I stare blankly at the swirling greenery as the bug bumps along the winding lake road, too engaged in my own thoughts to process the words coming out of his mouth after he admits his age.

Eighteen.

"Damnit," I mutter below my breath.

"What?"

I don't realize my softly spoken curse is audible over the whipping wind. The top is rolled back on the bug and my hair is slapping me across my face. I pull it into a messy bun and avoid his gaze.

"Nothing."

I learn he's a stubborn ass once we arrive at the grocery store. He argues and whines over my avoidance of purchasing brand name products, being the penny-pincher I've always been. We engage ourselves in a tug-of-war over a box of freaking Frosted Flakes that goes on for five minutes before I ungracefully bow out. I toss the blue box with the grinning tiger into the cart before walking away in a huff.

Jared follows me, cackling to himself as he pushes the squeaky cart behind me. He calls out that he wants soup tonight for supper, ignoring me as I argue over my shoulder about the sweltering heat and how it's too hot outside for soup.

We reach the canned goods aisle when *it* happens.

I'm standing on my tiptoes, reaching for a can above my head. I feel a rushing coolness of air drift across my exposed flesh when my shirt slightly lifts as I stretch to grab a can. My skin bursts into flames as I feel his warm fingers brush across my skin, his hands gripping tightly over my hips.

My heart is thumping so erratically. I feel as though it's about to burst. He presses himself against me, and I swallow dryly, gasping once his hard cock presses against the small of my back.

"What are you doing?" I manage to mumble, shocked I can even form the simple sentence.

The fingertips of his left hand dip below the waistband of my shorts, slipping below the string of my thong. His other hand leaves my body, easily reaching over my head and pulling a can from the shelf above. He hands it to me then places his free hand on my waist once more.

"Maybe I'll teach you how to cook tonight," he says, sounding thoughtful. "Then you can cook for me. I can't wait to *taste* what you have to offer. Would you like that, Sydney?"

My mouth opens and closes. I can hear him taking a deep breath, brushing his nose against the hair now hanging down at the nape of my neck, the messy bun somehow coming loose and slightly undone during our ride to the store.

"Of course you would," he says with a hint of teasing laughter in his voice. "You'd love for me to have a taste. The thing is, once I have a taste, I don't think I'll be able to stop. I'll want to keep tasting, and tasting, and tasting."

He thrusts his hard cock against me before releasing me, causing me to gasp and squirm. My legs feel weak, as though they're about to give out from beneath me, and I've never been so fucking turned on in my life.

I watch him as he walks away, practically sauntering as he grabs the buggy with the wild wheel that spins around. I stand alone in the canned goods aisle, holding a can of stewed tomatoes. He disappears around the corner, whistling to himself, uncaring that he's started something only he can stop.

The sexual innuendos go on day by day—the "accidental" brush against my back when I'm engaged in something, shocking me each time, or the twisting of simple words that turn me into mush. I know I should tell him to stop, but I can't. I can't tell him to stop, just like I can't stop the fantasies I have about him. It's not long before he knows exactly how attracted I am to him.

\*\*\*

I've been living in Biloxi for weeks. During this time I've maintained the same routine—waking up and drinking my coffee out on the pier, watching the sun as it rises in the distance, feeling Jared's eyes on my back from somewhere within the lake house behind me. I watch him as he stands over the stove, cooking eggs to perfection, laughing at the look of annoyance on my face at my inability to do so, before he gently places a plate in front of me.

The days are long when he's away at work. I spend them cleaning, reading, or simply staring out into the dark water, watching the fish and turtles break across the glassy surface, wondering about my future and how long I'll stay in this town so far away from my home.

My nights are spent with him, giggling and fighting over the remote control, trembling when he smirks and not-so-innocently brushes his fingers across my skin on occasion. I listen to him in rapt attention as he talks about his childhood, the stunts he and Ellie would pull. I drink in his carefree laugh, his wicked smile, his taunting eyes.

I find myself mesmerized by this young man.

When I'm all alone in my bedroom, long after the sun disappears, I think of him. I lie in bed tossing and turning, eventually lying on one side and staring through the window at the big, white moon.

The familiar butterflies flit in my stomach once his face flashes in my mind. I gnaw on my lip for a moment before tugging my sleep top off, tossing it and then my cotton shorts and panties to the floor.

I want him. I want him behind me, fucking me until I'm so exhausted I beg him to stop. I want his hard cock slamming into me as he pins me down on my bed. Just the thought of him sweaty and thrusting into me leaves me wet and throbbing. Before I know it I'm rolling onto my stomach, the image of him taking me from behind playing in my mind as I buck my hips against my own fingers, stroking myself.

My knees dig into the mattress, my fingers thrusting inside in a steady rhythm, harder and harder. My heart feels as though it will beat its way out of my chest. I cry out his name into my pillow as I come, then fall into an exhausted slumber, my fingers wet and sticky, a smile on my face.

\*\*\*

It's a muggy Saturday night filled with the sound of crickets and frogs singing in an unmarred harmony. We sit on the deck for a while, watching the sun disappear into the horizon, studying the sky streaked with purple and pink before returning to the cooler confines of the house. Jared joins me on the couch, sitting alarmingly close, jeans brushing against my bare skin below the hem of my sundress.

I sip a glass of wine, teasing him occasionally over his age and the fact that I'm a legal adult. Old enough to buy alcohol without even being carded anymore, I poke fun at him to help smother the fluttering in my chest caused by him sitting closely by my side.

"Why are you so obsessed with your age?" he asks, staring at me with his eyebrows slightly raised.

"I'm not obsessed with my age," I grumble. My wine glass suddenly looks fascinating.

"Yes, you are," he responds. "You bring it up all the time. I don't think you even realize when you're doing it."

I shrug and sigh, suddenly feeling a bit melancholy as I gulp down the last of the sweet liquid and place the empty glass on the coffee table.

I feel his gaze for a moment before he reaches in his pocket. The contents cause my mouth to drop open and he snickers at the way I gape at the small bag of weed.

"You smoke?" he asks, his grin mischievous.

"No," I whisper, remembering my list of things I want to try before I turn thirty. "Never."

I watch in awe as he breaks open a small cigar, dumping the tobacco in one corner of a large, unused ashtray on the coffee table and then rolling a blunt. I silently try to memorize the technique in case I ever need to use it. He leans back, sinking against the soft cushions of the couch. He finishes and glances at a lighter on the table, a lighter that is sitting closer to me. His eyes dart pointedly between me and the lighter.

I grab it, twist sideways and flick my thumb over the rough metal. His eyes never leave mine as I light the blunt and he takes a drag. I'm mesmerized by the sight of his cheeks hollowing out before he slowly releases the smoke into the air. It pours from his mouth, over his bottom lip and from his nose, swirling around his smirking face.

"You want?" he asks, cocking his head to the side. A slow grin curls on one corner of his mouth.

"Yeah," I whisper. "I want."

"If I give you this, what are you gonna give me in return?"

His cocky gaze transforms into a more serious one. My body burns under his stare, and my heart jumps into my throat. I say the words without a second thought.

"What do you want?"

Jared takes another drag. Then he tilts his head back, blowing the smoke into the air.

"To fuck you," he responds, meeting my bewildered stare at his admission, "and you're gonna let me, aren't you, Sydney?"

I open my mouth in shock, not even sure how to respond, but he doesn't give me time to speak.

"Come here."

Jared's expression is calm, even a bit playful, but his words are firm. He gestures to his lap and I suck in a deep breath. His pants are tented and I see the hard outline of his cock pressing against the faded fabric.

"You're eighteen," I mutter, unsure of what to do about the conflicting emotions brewing inside me. "Practically a kid."

He stares at me for a beat longer, his gaze boring into mine. Then he grabs my hand, placing it firmly on his long, hard cock.

"Do I feel like a kid?" he asks, guiding my hand up and down his length. "I'm a man. Get on my fucking lap and I'll prove it."

Every dirty fantasy I've had of this boy is nothing compared to this moment— the feeling of his cock beneath my hand as I unconsciously begin to stroke him through the fabric of his jeans, the dark, lusty eyes staring back at me, the thrill of his breathy moans breaking the heady silence of the room as my thumb encircles his engorged head.

A battle wages inside of me; good versus evil, right versus wrong. In the end he makes the decision for me, pulling me into his lap. I hover over him, my body humming in anticipation as he places his hands on the back of my bare thighs.

Jared pulls me further forward onto his lap, pressing me roughly against his hard length. I stare down at him with eyes wide open, feeling like a hesitant fucking virgin once again. His hands slide up my thighs under my sundress until he's cupping my ass in his hands.

"You know what 'shotgun' means, right?"

He laughs as I quirk an eyebrow, then he picks up the blunt and takes another drag. He drops the blunt back in the ashtray, gesturing for me to lean in.

I do. I press my mouth against his, taking in the smoke. My lips tingle and my body is set ablaze as his hand slips under my dress and back on my ass. I tilt my head back, watching the smoke billow through the air.

"Are you wet for me, baby?"

"Yes," I whisper, groaning as his fingers massage my flesh.

"Do you want me to fuck you?"

He smiles as I nod.

"Maybe later." He chuckles as my mouth drops open in surprise. "If you're a good girl."

I roll my eyes and make a move to stand, annoyed that he's leaving me wet and throbbing with no indication of relief in sight. He grips me harder, holding me in place, his eyes flashing dangerously.

"Don't walk away from me," he warns. "There are other ways I can make you feel good."

I freeze as his hands run up my sides beneath the dress, slipping the thin material over my head and then tossing it aside. His tongue darts out to wet his lips as he gazes at my bra-clad chest.

Leaning forward, he flicks his warm tongue against the fabric of my bra, tracing a slow, wet circle around my hardened nipple.

"Keep smoking," he murmurs against my breast.

I nod, hesitantly picking up the blunt, ignoring how foreign it feels in my hand. I take short drags between my moans as he sucks my nipple between his teeth. He releases it as I take another drag of the blunt.

Then he leans in to shotgun once more.

I press my lips against his, releasing the smoke from my lungs. He inhales but holds my head in place after doing so. The smoke rolls out of his mouth, around both of our lips. He languidly slips his tongue inside my mouth.

My fingers are entangled in his hair, gripping him in desperation as our tongues teasingly dart in and out of each other's mouths. I slowly begin to rock against his hard cock, groaning into his mouth as he grinds against me as well. Thrills of pleasure pulse through my body, his hard length roughly grazing the throbbing heat between my legs.

Jared pulls his mouth away from mine, licking and nibbling his way from my mouth, down my neck and back to my nipples as he tugs at my hair. I pick up the blunt once more, now almost gone. I smoke the remainder of it while he takes turns on my nipples, licking and sucking first one, then the other.

The weed slowly seeps into my system, flowing through my veins, and suddenly I'm floating. I grind my body against his, speeding up my movements as he squeezes my ass.

"Fuck, Jared." I gasp, grinding against him. "Please make me come."

"You want to come, Sydney?" he asks, running his tongue between my tits and back up my neck.

"Yes. Fuck, yes."

"I'll make you come," he says, sucking my bottom lip between his teeth. "But you're not gonna come in my lap. You're gonna come in my mouth."

A thrilling sensation twists in the pit of my stomach at his words. He pulls me from his lap until I'm standing on wobbly legs hovering over him. He gives me a satisfied grin, tugging my wet panties down my legs. He stares at my naked lower body for a moment, wetting his lips. Then he runs his hand up my calf to the bend of my knee, lifting my leg and placing it on the armrest of the couch.

"Can't wait," he groans, kneading my ass in his hands, pulling my pelvis forward. "Can't wait to taste you on my tongue."

I grasp his hair between my fingers so hard that my knuckles turn white, gasping as he buries his face between my legs. He gives me a long, greedy lick, from back to front, then does this again and again as I circle my hips.

"That's right, baby," he mumbles against my wet flesh. "Ride my fucking face. God, you taste so fucking good."

Jared's hungry, pleasure-filled words vibrate against my clit as he eats me. I pinch my nipples between my fingers, hissing as I gently tug at the hard peaks. I struggle to stand, my legs feeling boneless as he glides his tongue between them, teasing me with each gentle lick.

I need him inside me, yet he avoids this as he concentrates on my clit and lips. His tongue mercilessly swirls around my entrance occasionally, but never darts inside.

I gaze down at him and meet his eyes. The sight of this man with his face buried between my legs, licking me as his pink tongue sweeps in and out between my lips, is enough to make me come undone. Coming forcefully in his mouth, I grip his hair in my hands, pressing him roughly against my convulsing pussy.

He gives my sensitive nub one last nip before he pulls away. I drop my leg from the couch, hardly able to stand on my weakened limbs. He slides my panties up my legs until they're back in place. There's a smirk on his face as he leans back into the cushions gazing up at me, and I can't help but giggle and snort at the expression.

"You're just so proud of yourself, aren't you?" I giggle again, feeling the full effect of the weed buzzing in my blood.

"Maybe."

Gloating with a shrug, his eyes widen as I begin to sway on my feet. He's by my side in a second, grasping my waist, bringing back the memory of the day at the grocery store from within the deep recesses of my mind. I stare up at him glassy-eyed and giggling, laughing harder as the smirk returns stretching across his handsome face. He chuckles, shaking his head at me and helping me across the room.

We stumble up the stairs leading to my bedroom. I laugh as he practically drops me on the bed, landing beside me, gazing into my hazy eyes. His arrogant grin disappears, replaced with a tender expression. My laughter dies away, a crippling fear deep inside.

"I'm really tired," I stupidly blurt out, cringing at my blunt words.

I try to avoid his imploring eyes, but it's impossible. My heart drops as he stands up, a look of disappointment on his face.

"Get some sleep, Sydney."

I quietly nod, chewing on my bottom lip. Stepping away, he runs his fingers through his hair. His leg bumps against the computer desk near the bedroom door, and he glances down at it, his brow furrowing.

"What's this?" He picks a worn napkin up, his eyes darting across the faded words.

I'm suddenly too high, too exhausted, and too ashamed of myself to care that he's reading something very personal of mine.

"Things I want to do before I turn thirty."

"Watch a sunrise ... learn how to swim ... ride a motorcycle. You've never done these things before?"

"No, never."

He nods thoughtfully, placing the napkin back on the desk.

"Sweet dreams, Sydney," he whispers.

My eyes flutter and I quickly succumb to my exhaustion. The last thing I remember before drifting away is the feeling of warm lips placing a delicate kiss against my forehead.

# Chapter Five

I wake up groaning, the memory of the night before present even after the weed I smoked. Shame fills my chest with how I behaved last night, more like a child than a grown woman. Jared is barely fucking legal and I allowed him to touch me, to taste me, in a way only a *man* touches a woman. Glancing at the digital clock on my nightstand, I notice that it's seven o'clock. I bite my lip and cover my face with my hands, fully intending to hide out in my borrowed bedroom for at least forty-five minutes until Jared leaves for work.

Turns out I don't have to wait after all.

A rumbling sound growls from somewhere outside, so loud I can feel the floor trembling beneath me. I drag myself out of bed, edging across the room and hiding behind the curtains to look down below.

Jared emerges from the garage I didn't even realize is in use. The door has always been closed, and I've never seen Jared open it or park his truck inside. I watch in rapt attention as he slowly pulls out a sleek, deep red motorcycle. It's old, although I don't know how old. I don't even know the make or model, being green to motorcycles in general. All I know is that he's beautiful on it, straddling it and gunning the engine, peeling out of the long drive and disappearing into the pine-shaded distance.

I try to erase the memory of last night from my mind, but it doesn't go away. I scrub the house from top to bottom, even shampooing the dirty carpet until it looks new again. I wash clothes and clean the fridge. I pace around until the sun is gone, and he's still not home. A part of me is relieved he's not here. Avoidance isn't my middle name, but it could be. A bigger part of me is worried he regrets what happened last night, worried that he's not coming back until I'm gone and worried he might be hurt from riding the motorcycle.

I sit at the kitchen table long after dark, chewing my nails down to the nub. My eyes dart to the clock constantly, the methodical *tick-tick* driving me absolutely mad. I don't know who to call. I can't call *him*. We've never exchanged numbers. There's never been any need to. When he's not working he's by my side, warming not only my skin with his presence but also my heart, chipping away the ice-cold exterior that's developed there over the years. I've never met any of his friends. He's never mentioned his parents. As a matter of fact, there are no pictures of him or his family in this house, which I find odd and a little sad.

It's midnight when I hear the rumble of the motorcycle in the distance. It grows louder as he approaches and then dies completely after I hear him park it in the garage. When he walks through the door he freezes, looking like a deer caught in headlights as he meets my gaze.

"Where have you been?"

My voice is harsh and demanding. Bewilderment slips from his face and is quickly replaced with narrowed eyes.

"Out," he mutters. "Why?"

"Why?" I throw my hands up in frustration and stand. "I haven't seen nor heard from you all day."

The pink of his tightly pinched lips turns white with my confrontational tone. His eyes narrow into little slits, and he slams the door behind him, causing me to jump, shaking the walls with his anger.

"Since when do I have to answer to you? You're not my damn mother. I haven't answered to anyone in a long time, and I'm not gonna start now."

Something breaks inside me, tearing through my chest. My anger slips away at his defensive words. He's right. Not only am I *not* his mother, I'm not anyone *else* of significance to him either. One misspent night doesn't mean I can stake a claim on him, or he on me.

Isn't this what I wanted when I woke up this morning? To distance myself from him? To pretend last night never happened?

I turn away, shuffling toward the staircase to hide the tears spilling over my cheeks.

"Come back here." Jared quickly crosses the room and darts in front of me.

"It's fine," I whisper, trying to shove past him as I avoid his eyes.

"Fuck, are you *crying*?"

"Move," I groan as he blocks the staircase. "Just forget it."

"Why the fuck are you crying?"

"Because I thought you left," I shout. Wiping the tears from my face, I'm ashamed of showing such emotion in front of him. "I thought you *left*. I thought maybe you were *hurt*. I thought maybe you were *dead*. But you're right. I'm not your mother. It's none of my business where you go or what happens to you, right?"

He says nothing as I shove past him and dart up the stairs, but I can feel him. I can feel him on my heels. I can hear his soft breaths expelling from his chest. I try to shove my bedroom door shut behind me, but he pushes back against it, causing me to stumble slightly and the door to slam against the wall.

"You were worried about me?"

"Of course I was worried about you!"

I'm screaming now. Screaming and crying. Feeling like an idiot for being overly worried to begin with and feeling like a stupid woman for falling for this boy.

Because I have. I've fallen for this boy.

"Come here."

"No," I grumble stubbornly.

His eyes grow dark, and I panic a bit at the expression. My gaze darts between him and the door, calculating the distance and if I should make a run for it.

"Don't even think about it," he says, his voice stern.

"Don't tell me what to do, Jared. You're a fucking *child*."

Tension fills the air. The two of us glare at one another in mutual anger and frustration, but through it all I can feel it. I can feel the sexual energy bursting all around us, warming my belly.

I pull my bottom lip between my teeth and he stalks forward, tugging his shirt over his head. His tosses it to the floor, his eyes never leaving mine. The muscles on his defined upper body are tense in his anger. They jut back and forth, his chest heaving with each frustrated breath.

I back into the wall, terrified, yet aroused by the predatory look in his eyes.

I moan once his mouth attacks my own. Tossing my arms over his shoulders, I kiss him back fervently. He groans with the thrust of my tongue inside his mouth, grinding himself roughly against me. His hands slide down my body and then back up as he removes my shirt. He tugs the cups of my bra down below my breasts, exposing my curves and straining nipples.

Clutching my hand in his, he guides it to his jean-clad cock. I stubbornly refuse to stroke it, abandoning his mouth, my lips swollen from his desperate kisses.

He dismisses my silent refusal, guiding my hand over his swollen cock with one hand and unbuttoning my shorts with the other. They slide down my legs, and there's no time to react.

I gasp as his fingers immediately dip beneath my panties and push deep in my entrance, curling inside me.

"You can play stubborn all you want." He languidly traces his tongue around one nipple and then the other, pumping his fingers inside me. "Your body tells me all I need to know."

"We can't do this," I stutter. "What we're doing now, what we did last night ... I mean, fuck, Jared. I'm about to turn thirty. You're eighteen years old!"

*Oh, my God.*

*What am I doing?*

There's no weed or wine to blame for my actions, for allowing him to touch me so intimately. I twist away from him, forcing his fingers to slip from between my legs. Strong arms wrap around my waist as he draws me backwards against his hard chest. I curse him below my breath, struggling against him. He drops down on the bed, pulling me into his lap.

"Where the fuck do you think you're going?" he asks.

"Away from you."

"Is that really what you want?" he whispers in my ear, loosening his grip around me, releasing my arms. "You want to get away from me?"

I moan, pivoting my hips as he pulls my panties aside and brushes his fingers against me.

"I'm not letting you go, Sydney," he says, stroking my clit, his cock jutting against my ass. "And I don't think you really want me to."

Whimpering, I roll my hips while he lazily massages my clit. He lightly tweaks my nipples, capturing them tightly between his fingers, pulling each one away from my body before releasing it.

"After I fuck you," he says, running his tongue from my shoulder, up my neck, and across my jaw, "you'll never want to leave."

Two fingers slide deeply inside me, then back out, traveling from my entrance, across my lips, to my swollen nub, then back again in a steady rhythm.

"Jared," I gasp, crying out when he bites my neck just over my jugular.
"Fuck."

"Fuck is right." He grunts, forcing me to stand then shoving me onto the bed. "If you really don't want this, tell me now."

I gaze up at him, at the intensity in his eyes. I reach out, slowly unbuttoning his fly and tugging his jeans down. His boxers catch on his thick cock as I slide them down as well.

A deep shudder rustles through his body as I wrap my hand around his length and begin to suck. The two of us watch one another as I pleasure him, moaning around him when he hits the back of my throat.

"I need you, Syd," he rasps in a throaty moan.

I'm pushed onto my hands and knees in a very primal pose that thrills me to the core. My body is throbbing with want as he slips the thong from my legs. The head of his cock presses against me. He slips the tip just inside and our groans fill the muggy air.

Sliding out and barely easing in once more, he slowly stretches me, my body accommodating his thick length.

Then he's inside me, pivoting his hips, his skin slapping against mine. I lean on my elbows as he grasps my waist, pulling me flush against him. Resting my thighs against his, I lock my ankles behind his back, craving him deeper. He begins to move in slow, needy thrusts, hitting me just right with each stroke.

I turn my head to watch as he enters me from behind, gasping as he thrusts and fills me. The expression on his face is one I won't soon forget: pure, unbridled pleasure. His deft fingers grip my waist, pulling me against him, his eyes gliding over the curves of my body. When he catches me watching him he scoops me up, wrapping one arm under my breasts.

My knees hit the bed as he thrusts up, pulling me flush against his sweaty chest. I gasp at the new sensation and he palms my full breasts then presses one long finger against my clit. His movements become more persistent. Jutting upward inside me, bouncing me on his lap, he murmurs dirty words in my ear.

"Do I feel like a man, baby?"

"God, yes." I whimper as he gently tweaks my sticky, swollen nub. He pinches my nipple between his long fingers, rolling it deliriously slow.

"Who makes you feel this good?"

"You do," I moan. "Oh, God."

When he tugs gently at my clit I come undone. The frenzied knot of heat contained in the depths of my belly seeps into my veins. Crying out, I bounce on his lap, desperate to ride out the most intense orgasm I've ever had.

"Do you want me to come inside you, Sydney?" he asks, sucking my earlobe between his lips. The thought of him filling me causes excitement to jar me. Liquid heat bubbles inside my belly.

"Yes," I say. "Please, come inside me."

Pushing my upper body down onto the bed, his body jerks erratically. The soft sounds of our sex resonate through the air, the slap of his body pounding against mine. Then he delves so deep, so furiously, that the familiar burn begins again, flashing through my stomach.

I come uncontrollably, burying my face in the soft, downy sheets. Hot liquid pours from inside me, spilling out and trickling against my throbbing flesh. He spasms as well, jerking his body against mine and grinding out my name.

***

"I shouldn't have made you worry," he says later that night.

The sound of his abnormally soft voice shatters the silence of the room. The bed shifts with the turn of his body as he rolls onto his side and openly stares at me. I make a move to tug the covers over my exposed body, but he stops me, pulling the duvet down and exposing my bare breasts once more. He trails one finger across the curve of my right breast before slowly encircling my nipple. I bat his curious hand away before he can distract me any further.

"No, you were right," I respond. "Your comings and goings are none of my business. I overreacted."

"Why did you think I left?" he questions, sounding slightly wounded by the insinuation. "I get that you thought I was hurt. It was a shit thing to do, not coming home until midnight, but I didn't think you'd care."

"Of course I care." I bite my lip a bit before continuing. "My mother left me when I was a kid. My friends all graduated high school and left town before the ink was dry on their diplomas. Every boyfriend I've had has bailed on me. I just ... I just don't want to lose you too."

I instantly feel pathetic with my admission. I turn away from him, lying on my left side and willing my eyes to stay dry. When did I turn into such an emotional wreck? Is it possible to have a mid-life crisis at thirty?

The longer he doesn't speak the worse I feel. I sit up in bed and run my fingers through my tangled hair before trudging to the bathroom, refusing to look his way. I lock the door behind me and press my back against it. Sliding to the floor, I let the tears fall with me.

"Sydney," he murmurs. "Sydney, open the door."

"I'm gonna take a shower," I say in the strongest voice I can muster, shaking my head and wiping the tears away. "I'll be out in a few minutes."

"Open the door, Syd. Don't shut me out."

"Jared …"

"Open the door or I'll break it down. It's up to you."

I mutter a curse below my breath, stand, and open the fucking door. He shuffles past me, still naked, and the sound of the shower spray hitting the tiled stall floor fills the room. Steam follows as well, and soon the room is nothing but a misty swirl of fog, water and him. Wordlessly, he laces his fingers through mine and steps into the shower, guiding me behind him.

The scent of my strawberry shampoo fills the air as he washes my hair, massaging my scalp. I moan at the sensation, the pure pleasure that it sends quaking through my bones.

My soapy loofah slowly travels my body. He works it across my skin, teasing my breasts by skimming his thumb over my nipples. His gaze is sexual yet tender, and something else is there as well although I can't quite place the emotion.

I press my hands against his chest, running my fingertips over the hard surface, memorizing every curve of muscle. His abs clench when I travel lower, and I can't help but smile at the discovery of him being ticklish.

He doesn't smile back. His eyes are dark and filled with that unspoken, unrevealed emotion. Long fingers wrap around my wrists, halting my movements as I travel lower.

Draping my arms over his shoulders, he presses me further into the spray of water, resting his forehead gently on mine. We stay that way until the water grows cold and we're both shivering.

It's not until I'm standing near my bedroom window, wrapped in a soft towel and staring down at the lake below that he finally speaks from where he's perched on the edge of my borrowed bed.

"My parents are dead," he whispers, his voice tinged with pain. "Ellie was left to raise me alone. It was hard on her giving up so much to take care of her kid brother. I think that's why she took off after my high school graduation. I'm alone too, Sydney."

"Oh, Jared," I murmur.

I cross the room and join him on the edge of the bed. Running my fingers through his damp hair, I'm mesmerized by the softness of it. My heart crumbles as I watch his face harden as he forces back an emotion I'm so familiar with myself. He turns and gazes at me, meeting my eyes and cupping his hand on my cheek. His slightly calloused thumb makes contact with my bottom lip and I tremble.

"I'm alone in this fucking house that reminds me of *them* and Ellie, and *fuck*. I hate this place. I've hated this place for years. Then you show up and I don't hate it so much anymore. Last night ... *goddamn*. Last night was amazing, but then I saw the doubt in your eyes and it scared me. It *still* scares me."

"Why does it scare you?"

"Because you'll leave too."

Heartache and disappointment etches his voice, causing tears to well in my eyes. He stands and angrily paces around the room. I pull the towel tighter around me as I watch his lithe movements. He snatches my wrinkled napkin from the desk and waves it in the air.

"Tell me the truth." Towering over me, he hands me the list. "Are you leaving when you finish this list? Are you going back to Oregon?"

I take the list from him, staring down at the few wishes remaining, the few wishes crossed off.

"Maybe," I whisper, staring up into his defeated eyes as his shoulders slump. "Jared, where are you going in the fall?"

"College."

"Right." I nod and force a small smile. "You told me you were going to college. You have your entire life ahead of you. You should live it, not waste it on me."

"You think me caring about you is a waste?" he asks with disgust in his voice.

"Yes. I have nothing going for me. I'd hold you back, Jared. I can't do that. I care about you too much to hold you back."

The list grows hazy as my eyes cloud over. He takes it from my hands, and I stare down at the floor in numb silence until he speaks.

"How long do I have?"

"What do you mean?" I wrinkle my eyebrows in confusion and finally glance up into his eyes. Those eyes are no longer worried or troubled.

They're determined and full of confidence.

"How long until your birthday?" he asks, carefully folding the napkin in half. "How long until you leave?"

"Fourteen days," I murmur.

He appears to mull this over for a moment before his solemn face turns up into an eager grin.

"Can I help you check off your list?"

I raise my eyebrows as the seriousness of our conversation slips away, but I quickly brush his odd change in attitude aside, blaming it on his youth.

"Sure." I shrug, my stomach growing slightly queasy at the thought of the remaining wishes scrawled across that napkin. "If you want to."

# Chapter Six

"I can't believe I'm doing this." I gasp, cringing slightly as I feel Jared's hands leave my back.

With my ears full of water, I can't hear anything he says, but I can hear his boisterous laugh. I lie floating on my back, feeling lighter than ever before in my life.

I float for a long time, not bothered by the tortuous sun beating down upon my body, unconcerned by the beads of sweat forming on my forehead and stinging my eyes.

I'm floating.

I'm floating.

I'm lightness and darkness and air.

I'm everything not constrained and hinged down by life, by the toils and troubles of earth.

I'm floating.

He floats beside me. Our limbs brush against each other occasionally. There's a wistful smile on his face. We watch the fat, white clouds drift across the brilliant, blue sky. I wonder what he's thinking about, but I don't ask, choosing to let him live in his peaceful thoughts for the time being.

Over the past week we've slowly worked our way through my list. One last thing remains. One last thing I need to accomplish in my life before my birthday, but I've put it off, too terrified to accomplish it.

Riding a motorcycle.

I'm no longer necessarily scared of the vehicle, no longer terrified of the ride. I'm scared of what comes next, because once I've accomplished this goal there's nothing left to keep me here in Biloxi. There's nothing tying me down to this place which has grown so close to my heart.

Nothing but him, and he is everything to me.

Everything.

Neither of us has mentioned me leaving since that night. It's a subject left unspoken, although I continue to feel his desperation for me to stay in everything he does. I feel it when we make love at night. Sometimes he's gentle, and other times he's not, slamming into me and clutching me against his body as though he's trying to get lost inside of me.

I *want* to leave him.

I want him to go to college, graduate, find a girl his own age and settle down. I want him to sow his wild oats because he hasn't. He's eighteen and works all the damn time. When he's not working he's spending time with me, a woman over ten years his senior. Our time is spent checking off my fucking list and spoiling his last summer before he heads off to college.

I *don't* want to leave him.

I want to stay with him forever, until the end of our days. I want to wake up and make him coffee. I want to throw together a simple lunch of a sandwich and chips in a brown paper bag and shove it in his hands as he leaves for work. I want to hear him tease me relentlessly for my lack of cooking skills. I yearn to fall asleep with him forever like I do now, with his arm wrapped around my waist, pressing soft kisses to my bare shoulder as he spoons me.

I want to marry him.

I want to have his children.

Gasping, I fall under, taking one last breath before the lake consumes me. Water cascades around me, encasing me while I sink into the lake. Emerging in a panic, I sputter and cough, trudging against the silty lake bottom. He's behind me in a matter of seconds, grasping my arm, his hand slipping from my wet skin once I yank away from him.

"Sydney." His voice is edged with worry. "Sydney, what's wrong? Are you hurt? Sick? What happened?"

"Yes," I moan, suddenly feeling it in the pit of my stomach—the queasy feeling of guilt and remorse intertwined with hurt and want. "I feel sick."

I climb onto the pier and grab a towel, half-assed drying myself and running across the sun-blistered wood. My heart is hammering erratically, threatening to beat right out of my chest, and I'd let it. I'd let it flutter away into the wind because maybe I wouldn't feel the way I do every moment I'm with him.

Jared leaves me alone the rest of the night, only interrupting my self-loathing to bring me homemade tomato soup and cornbread. I stay in my bedroom curled in a ball on my bed, guilt consuming me with his thoughtful gesture. He quietly murmurs that it was his grandmother's recipe before softly pulling the door closed behind him.

In fact, he leaves me alone the next few days. I sleep alone at night, torturing myself by constantly weighing my options, convincing myself that this is for the best. I'm doing the right thing. I'll leave and let him be.

He's young.

He'll move on, find another girl, an actual *girl*, not a thirty-year-old woman.

\*\*\*

Jared comes to me the night before my birthday.

The creak of the door across the hall alerts me of his presence. The soft padding of feet over the carpet in the hallway might fall on deaf ears where others are concerned, but not me.

God knows I've missed him. I've been waiting for him, yearning for him, night after night. Too stubborn and set in my ways, my selfish pride burrowed deep inside my chest, I've kept my distance. Hurting him will kill me, and I will. I will hurt him by leaving.

And if I decide to stay, I will hurt him even worse.

Living with Jared any longer would be a greedy decision on my part. He's eighteen, a man who's not yet experienced life, no matter how much pain he's seen in the past few years. We're two damaged souls, spiraling out of control and crashing into one another, resulting in an explosion of emotions. The pain and anger we feel from the abandonment of our loved ones binds us together, but is that all there is? Is that enough to form a healthy, functioning relationship?

*No.*

Turning on my side and facing the window, I pretend not to hear him. I pretend not to hear his soft breaths, the rustle of the sheets beside me. I pretend not to notice the shift of the mattress under his knees, but I can't control the way my body responds to him. A needy shudder races through me, traveling from where he brushes my hair from my shoulder and all the way to my toes. His warm breath washes over me, his tender kisses peppering my shoulder and gliding along the arch of my neck.

Jared's natural, sexual domination is magical, a characteristic that's appealed to me from the beginning. But this—the way he kisses me now, slow and earnest, his tongue barely peeking from his mouth to tease my skin—seems much more intimate than any way he's touched me before. Something warm, something wet, slips down the swell of my cheek. I'm quick to swipe it away, to brush it aside and pretend those tears never existed.

Sighing my name against my skin, he kisses his way along my jawline until he reaches the corner of my mouth. Warm fingers tickle my belly with their light touch, the work-worn pad of his thumb rubbing soothing circles around my navel. Rolling onto my back, I bite my lip, focusing on the way his chest muscles flex as his hands dig into the mattress on either side of me. My legs have parted without thought or reason, my body's natural reaction to this man.

There's no thickness of hair dusting his chest, no excessive brawn to his sculpted body, but there are also no signs of childhood roundness, no youthful weight clinging to his bones. Tawny arms and tight, defined abs clench and release with each deep breath he takes. His weighted stare forces my gaze from the hint of a waistband peeking from his sleep pants. A broken man hovers above me, an aching confusion and tender longing swimming in his irises.

Cupping my hand behind his neck, I bring his face down to mine and part my lips, allowing his tongue to slip inside my mouth. Stroking his tongue against mine he moans, dropping his weight to his elbows. Our pelvises collide, our mutual, throbbing need evident in the way we thrust against one another, both groaning with the friction. Gradual and unhurried, his hands drift up the sides of my ribs beneath the thin cotton of my tank, pushing the material up and over my breasts. Hot, humid breaths spill over my nipples, mixing with the coolness of the ceiling fan swinging lazily overhead.

Anticipation spreads like wildfire in my body, stoked by the heat of his mouth along the curves of my breasts. He catches my eye, his pink tongue sweeping over one rosy peek and leaving a trail of saliva in its wake. Closing my eyes, my head falls back against my pillow and my thighs lock around his waist. Hooking my ankles behind his back, I pull him down, wanting him closer, *needing* him closer. Our bodies meld together, his teeth lightly scraping my nipple as he begins to suck. Each swallow draws my nipple deeper between his teeth, his tongue flicking it inside his mouth and sending a rush of desire through my body. Rolling my hips, I slide my heat against his length, desperate for a release in any way I can find it.

And find it I do. I come hard, dry humping him like the teenager I'm not, like the teenager I never was.

Jared moves to the other nipple, teasing it the way he teased the one now swollen from his tongue, bruised by his teeth. Sweet, sweet pain is what he causes me, physically and emotionally. Battling my pride the past few days seems like a distant memory. The roaming hand dipping inside my panties turns my mind to mush, my memory into a blurry haze. Nothing matters as he strokes my inner lips, his touch so soft, *too* fucking soft. I want his desperate touch, his dominating, forceful way of taking what he wants from my body.

But that man never appears.

Fingers ease inside me, delving deeper than they ever have before. Unmoving, he stays there, buried inside, his shuddering breath unsteady against my mouth. Pressing the pad of his thumb against my clit, he rocks his hand. A cry echoes off the walls of my borrowed bedroom. I don't even realize the cry is my own, not until the cries transform into pleading whimpers. His hair tickles my face as he glances down my body, watching himself work his fingers beneath my panties.

Tingles and throbs turn into a mess of quivering twitches, my orgasm threatening my body once again. His fingers slip from inside me, causing an unsatisfied moan to break free from my chest. Crawling down my body, he peels my underwear from my legs, never hesitating as I twist my fingers in his hair and guide his mouth where I crave him the most.

Jared places his hands on the back of my thighs, parting my legs wider and holding pressure there. Each time his tongue flickers against me, my legs jerk and my hips roll forward, forcing myself against his mouth. Moans rumble from his throat, vibrating against me. The sound and pulsation undulates the need inside me. One last shudder and my body spasms, my mouth falling open with a silent scream of pleasure muffled by my own gasp.

He enters me fluidly. Distracted by my orgasm, I don't have time to fathom what he's done, not even realizing he's slid out of his sleep pants and boxers. Stilling on top of me, he seeks out my mouth before he pulls out of my wet depths, only to bury himself inside me once more. In an agonizing, lazy rhythm, we make love.

Our mouths leaving one another is rare. On the occasion they do, it's only long enough to take a deep, staggering breath. I can't look at him, not when he's staring at me like I hold the sun, like I'm the ocean and the sand and everything that I'm not and never will be.

Sweat gathers on our bodies. The warmth of the day lingers behind, the muggy air unconcerned with the swirl of the fan blades above. The slickness of my thighs tightening around his waist feels so right, as though he's meant to be here, captured between my legs, bumping a place hidden inside of me with each stroke of his length.

Caressing my mouth with his own, I feel the tightness in his abdomen, the firmness of his grasp as he cups my ass with one hand. A fleeting thought flutters through my mind, and I push his chest with my palm, forcing his mouth to break away from mine.

Forehead bunched, he stares down at me, the pivot of his hips slowing until it stops altogether. Unlocking my ankles from around him, I guide him to his back, giggling at the wideness in his eyes, the smile on his face.

"Is this okay?" I whisper, the first words spoken between us tonight.

"More than okay. It's just ... I've never had ..."

Words die away with the sway of my hips, replaced with his startled moan. Pride rushes through me, the emotion spurred on by the awe in his eyes. Of all the things he's done before me, all the things on my list he's experienced and I hadn't, this is something he's not familiar with. This is something I've done, something I've experienced, something I can share with the boy below me, the *man* below me.

Jared's hands run up the front of my thighs, grasping my waist long enough to allow him to thrust upward one, two times, before traveling over my ribs. His thumbs flick across my puckered nipples, the pink buds directly linked to the heated core between my legs. One hand remains, palming and squeezing my breast, the other drifting down my belly. Grinding my teeth together, I struggle to ignore the urgent need between my legs, wanting to hold on to this feeling as long as possible. His thumb sweeps across my clit, nudging back the sensitive hood. He massages me in torturous, lazy circles, groaning when I circle my hips above him.

"What are you doing to me?" he whispers. "What have you *done* to me?"

I cease my actions at the sound of his choked out words, but he never pauses from massaging my clit. Studying his face, I seek out the confusion tied to his staggering voice, but find none. Only reverence and longing lie there in his steady gaze and I drink it in, the sight of adoration, the sound of his gasping breath pushing me over the edge. Spasms overcome my body, my inner muscles squeezing and convulsing around him.

"Do you feel that?" I whisper, still twitching. "Do you feel what you do to me?"

He says nothing, only bringing both his hands to my waist and driving himself upward inside me. The lazy pace we once kept no longer exists. Our erratic, jerky rhythm takes its place, the desire to fulfill his own need evident in the way he plunges into me, as though I'm about to disappear, leaving him behind. Liquid heat fills me, warming my already burning body. Jared continues to thrust upward after his orgasm, eventually softening inside me. Our heavy breaths fill the air, although not quite as heavy as the uncertain stare between us, or as weighted as the dread clouding my chest.

"Come here." He runs his hands up my body, dragging his fingers through my hair. "Kiss me."

Leaning down, I allow him to kiss me, more as a distraction than anything else. The *thump-thump* of my heart nearly tears my chest in half, threatening to kill what is left of me. Wrapping his arms around me, we fall to one side, kissing and not speaking, eyes sometimes open and seeking. Fear grips me, because I know what just happened between us. And I hate myself for it. I hate myself for allowing him to make love to me, for allowing myself to make love to *him*, knowing I'm about to leave.

# Chapter Seven

Thirty years old.

That's what I am today.

I'm thirty years old. I sit on the deck and sip my coffee, watching the sun rise, wondering where things went so wrong in my life, wondering what the next chapter holds for me. My spoon clinks against the mug. I swirl the contents around, humming in appreciation of the taste of the sweet liquid I no longer take black—not after Jared introduced me to the wonders of his favorite coffee liqueur.

My suitcase is waiting when I reach the front door, now covered in buttons and stickers from my travels across the country. I packed it last night with nimble fingers and a numb mind. I pick it up now, hating the way it feels in my hands, like failure and defeat. But there are things waiting to be done. Bills have been left unpaid. Rent is due on a house I don't miss. Phone calls need to be returned to my father, a man who once kept his emotions bottled away, but has since decided to open up once his only child is hundreds of miles away. I grab the suitcase in one hand and emerge from the house, pausing on the weathered deck.

Jared leans against his motorcycle, legs crossed in front of him. Shades cover his eyes, but they can't hide the grim expression on his face. I slowly approach him, tossing the suitcase into the passenger seat of my tiny car, gravel crunching beneath my feet. The moroseness leaves his face once I'm standing just a whisper away. His pink lips turn into a small smile and he speaks three words, a demand, not a request.

"Ride with me."

I nod before his words are even fully absorbed inside my head. Trepidation sinks in the closer I step to the daunting vehicle. This is what I've wanted, the last thing on my list, but I've repressed the urge to finish what I started. My subconscious is most likely to blame. I've been completely aware of the fact that once the last wish is checked off my list, I'll have no excuse to stay in Biloxi.

Jared pushes himself from the bike and turns. Gripping the handles in his hands, he tosses one leg over the bike, upheaving it beneath him and straddling the heavy machine.

I carefully climb on behind him, pressing my body snugly against his. I relish the sensation of his abdominal muscles tensing and flexing under my fingers once I wrap my arms around his waist. Tension melts with the knowledge of him so close, knowing he'd never allow me to be harmed. He guns the engine and the bike roars to life beneath us. The sound and the vibrations travel straight to my core, causing me to press myself even more firmly against him.

We're gone, weaving down the winding lake road with the wind against our faces. My heart is in my throat with each sharp turn he takes, the vehicle dangerously slanted sideways toward the road below us. He glides us across the earth with skill and determination, expertly handling the motorcycle as though he's been riding it his entire life.

When we hit the intercoastal highway I relax somewhat, letting the whipping wind care for my sweaty hands, easing up on my grip of his body before releasing him altogether.

My arms are in the air, fingers spread out, reaching for nothing, yet everything. It's nothing like drifting in a weed-induced happiness or floating on my back in the murky water or buying a convertible top car more suitable for a teenage girl.

It's like flying, yet I'm not flying alone. I'm flying with *him*, and it feels right, like I was made to feel the freedom of the wind in my hair and my body nestled so closely to his.

We pull into a near-empty parking lot by a deserted stretch of beach some distance from the highway. Jared cuts the engine and the rumbling motorcycle dies, the monstrous growling and yearning sound instantly fading away, replaced with the crooning of seagulls and happy children playing on a distant surf.

Jared silently pulls me from the bike and toward a nearby, empty pavilion. We stroll hand in hand across the simmering lot, dipping beneath the shade. I start to sit, but he drops onto the picnic table first, pulling me down with him as he goes.

I sit between his legs as he presses himself against me, burying his face in the crook of my neck, breathing in my scent. We watch the children play for a while and I can't help but wonder what's going through his mind. Does he have the same ridiculous thoughts of what it would be like if we were to have children? Are his eyes closed1 behind me, his head filled with images of our sun-kissed babies with plump legs dancing and squealing along the shoreline?

I shake my head, tearing my gaze away from the shore. My irrational sense of longing fades away, my new focus on his hands clasping mine. They tremble slightly, although the late summer sun still hangs in the air giving enough heat to keep us warm. His soft lips pepper delicate kisses along my collarbone as he works his way to my ear, then he breathes the words I've never been told before.

"I'm in love with you, Sydney."

My chest tightens at his words, at the softness and sincerity in his sweet voice.

"I know it's not what you want to hear," he says, "but it's the truth. You probably think I'm too young to know what love is, but I'm not. I feel it in my chest. It's crippling and painful and fucking wonderful and horrible all at once, but I can't live without it, not now that I've experienced it.

"And I'm not letting you leave me. I can't stop you from leaving Biloxi, but know that I'll follow you. I'll follow you across Mississippi, across The Dirty Thirty and all the way back to Flint, Oregon. I'll follow you anywhere, Sydney, because I love you. I want to spend the rest of my life loving you."

I'm rendered speechless by his words. My body sinks against him as he strokes my arms beneath his hands, lightly massaging my skin. He says nothing, waiting for my response with more patience than a man his age should have, with more dignity than I deserve.

"Biloxi is nice," I mumble, watching the low-rising waves lap against the shore. "I really love it here."

He hums in agreement, gently kissing the sensitive skin just below my ear.

"I love trying new things with you," I add. He nods against my neck, his lips now running teasingly along my jawline. "I'd miss sleeping next to you at night and waking up beside you. I love watching your face when you first wake up in the morning, the way you always look surprised to see me staring back."

"What else?" he murmurs against the edge of my mouth.

"I love your laugh," I whisper, tears pricking the corners of my eyes. "I love the way the corners of your eyes crinkle when you smile, the way you tease me, the way you make love to me."

"Is that all?" he asks, pressing a chaste kiss to my lips as I whisper my last confession.

"I love *you*," I say breathlessly, feeling the curl of his lips against mine as they draw into a smile. "I've fallen in love with you, Jared."

The hard, rigid muscles of his chest pressed against the curve of my back stiffen for a moment and then relax. We hold one another as the sun shifts in the horizon, slowly dipping far beyond the white sand and lazy waves.

There are no plans made, no silly little lists. There's just me, him and the waves crashing in the distance.

All my downfalls, every single regret washes away with the pull of the tide, at least for now, because why worry? Why should anyone waste a single moment in time worrying about things we have no control over, such as age or the past?

Or falling in love.

**Want to follow Jessa Kaye for future publications? You can find her, along with author L.C. Morgan, at**

www.literoticaontherun.com

*About the Author:*

*Jessa Kaye lives in a small, rural community tucked beneath the tall pines of the Deep South. She enjoys sipping sweet tea, listening to The Civil Wars on her iPod, and pecking away on her laptop. Born with a mind full of stories, her love of writing was rekindled once she stumbled upon fanfiction. Encouraged by a friend to read the stories posted on Twilighted, she immediately fell in love with a world she didn't know existed. Years later she decided to try her hand at writing again, a hobby she'd once had as a thirteen-year-old girl. Instead of being enthralled by the keys on a typewriter, Jessa learned to love her laptop ... especially since she doesn't have to use White-Out to erase any mistakes.*

*When she's not busy writing you can find her at work, or chasing her three children around the house, or maybe burning her husband's supper.*

Made in the USA
Middletown, DE
08 December 2014